The Berenstain Bears
PLAY BALL

Stan & Jan Berenstain

Cartwheel
B·O·O·K·S®

SCHOLASTIC INC.
New York Toronto London Auckland Sydney

It's spring fever time
in Bear Country, friends—
a slow, easy time
that the Bear family spends
doing nothing more taxing
than gently relaxing.

Look! There's Mama Bear
taking her ease,
quietly shelling
early green peas.

The Berenstain Bears
PLAY BALL

ISBN 0-590-95734-1

12 11 10 9 8 7 6 5 4 3 2 1   8 9/9 0 1 2 3/0

Printed in the U.S.A.   08
First Scholastic printing, May 1998

That lump beside her,
Papa Bear, if you please,
needs no excuse
to catch a few **Z**'s.

But, hey! What's this—
a whirling hubbub,
roughly the size
of a smallish she-cub?

It's Sister Bear!
Just look at her go!
What a performance!
What a show!

But, did Papa Bear notice
Sister Bear's caper?
Humph. Not a chance.
He hardly noticed
the afternoon paper.

But then Papa stretched,
woke with a yawn,
and checked the headline to see
what was going on.

"Did you see it?" he cried.
"A classic home run swing!
A future hall of famer!
An absolute sure thing!"

A quick look at the paper
confirmed Mama's worst fears.
The disease that strikes terror
whenever it appears.

Spring fever had given way
to something much more serious.
Papa was, by now,
practically delirious
with the dreaded disease—

known as . . .
Little League fever!

Mama knew she had to stop him.
It was like a fever in the blood.
She really had no choice.
She had to nip it in the bud.

"I'm sure you'll agree," said Mama to Papa,
in her most reasonable tone.
"That it's wrong to pressure children.
They must do things on their own.
It's very wrong for dads
to relive their hopes and dreams
by making little children
play on baseball teams."

Said Papa Bear to Mama,
"I couldn't agree with you more.
I have nothing but contempt
for the sort of windy bore . . .

"who makes defenseless children
do things they'd rather not.
They are selfish and unfeeling,
a thoroughly bad lot.

They are pitiful and sad,
an absolute disgrace . . .
to the sacred name of DAD!

On the other hand, however,
if a lad should want to play,

"it wouldn't do at all
to stand in the youngster's way."

So Papa put the question
as Brother sauntered by.
"Would you like to go out
for baseball, son?
It's up to you, of course,
but it might be lots of fun."

A simple "I guess so"
was all that Papa got,
but it was all that Papa needed.
He departed like a shot—

up into the tree house attic
for his ancient paraphernalia
and was back down in a jiffy
in full baseball regalia.

Now, Brother liked baseball.
He often played it
with his buddies.
But they didn't need advice
from a lot of fuddy-duddies
because when all
was said and done,
grown-ups forgot that baseball
was intended to be fun.

So when Brother's buddies
called on him to play,

out of feeling for his dad,
he sent them on their way.

"There's no stopping him now," said Mama with a sigh. "I see that wild and crazy look in Papa's eye."

"How fortunate you are, my lad, how cleverly you chose your dad.

When it comes to baseball, I have expert knowledge, having starred in sandlot, school, and college.

I'm a student of its lore, statistics, and traditions."

I'm a master of all eleven positions.

ELEVEN?

"Er, Papa, I don't mean to get out of line. But, doesn't baseball call for nine?"

"Just checking to see if you're paying attention. Now, some baseball basics worthy of mention.

Observe closely —

the ball,

the bat,

the glove,

the hat.

So under **Mama's** watchful eye, small Sister Bear **did** give it a try.

She caught the ball.

She twirled the bat.

She pounded the glove

and tossed the cap.

But, did Papa take note
of Sister Bear's skills?
No way! Girls were creatures
of ruffles and frills,
having nothing to do
with baseball skills.

It was crystal clear,
at least to mother,
that Sister's skills
were clearly better
than those of Brother.

Now Papa
loved Sister Bear.
But, as for baseball,
it was as though
she wasn't there!

"Now, now, my dear.
Let us not interfere
with Brother's budding
baseball career.

So let us be
on our way!
Little League tryouts
start today!

The time has come
to give it a whirl,
to show them how
you hit and hurl!"

So Sister Bear
was left behind.
She couldn't pretend
that she didn't mind.

She minded terribly,
terribly much.
She loved Papa Bear,
but why was he such
a such-and-such!

She went to Mama,
and her early green peas,
"Would you tell me something,
Mama, please?
Why doesn't Papa
give *me* a whirl?
Is it," she sobbed,
"because I'm a girl?"

But, alas, Mama had no salve or ointment to ease her daughter's disappointment.

Brother Bear was betwixt and between, as he observed the Little League scene, where dozens of noisy Little League dads were busily signing up Little League lads. But as he took the pen and signed, a question formed in Brother Bear's mind. Who was Little League for? Father or son? It's *cubs* who are supposed to be having the fun.

SIGN UP HERE

It was a wonderful field,
with a real home plate,
and painted white lines.
Oh, it would have been great
to play on a field
so brand spanking new.
There was just one problem:
too many grown-ups spoiled the view.

There was a constant buzz
among the dads,
all bragging about
their Little League lads.
Said Pa, "My lad's best.
He's really super.
And after I teach him
my secret pitch,
the super-de-looper . . ."

Brother liked baseball.
But, truth to tell,
he had other
interests as well.

So, when a beautiful
butterfly lit,
Brother Bear set about
studying it.

It was more than
Papa could stand.
"Son, nature *is* wonderful.
But on the other hand,
if you're going to achieve
glory and fame,

you're going to have to
KEEP YOUR MIND ON THE GAME!

"Son, you don't see
the major league guys
like Babe Bruin and Ken Grizzly, Jr.
hanging around with *butterflies*!

Now, here's how to throw
my pitch of pitches.
You place your fingers
along the stitches.

"Dad, if it's all
the same to you,
I've sort of got
some things to do.

And since you're
tied-up, anyway,
I'll see you
later on, today."

"Come back!" cried Pa.
"There's more to be done!
You must learn to bunt
and how to perform
the hit-and-run!"

But Brother had enough
of baseball studies.
He needed some fun time
with his buddies.

"Please," said Mama,
as she helped Papa unwind,
"I don't wish to seem unkind.
But it really
isn't fair,
the way you're treating
Sister Bear."

But her protest fell
upon deaf ears.
For Papa, his mind aboil
with concerns and fears

that Brother, pressured
by his peers,
was headed for trouble,
up to no good.

He followed Brother
into the wood!

What was it with Brother?
Why had he fled?
What was going on
in that boy's head?

Pesky bugs
tickled Pa's nose.
Grasping twigs
tore at his clothes.

The woods got thicker
and thicker still,
with thorns as sharp
as a porcupine's quill.

"Uh-oh!" said Papa.
"It's worse than I thought!
You do things in caves
so as not to get caught!"

Papa Bear knew
what he had to do—
learn the secret
of Brother Bear's rendezvous.

He pressed into the cave.
It was quite a squeeze.
But within the darkness,
he felt a breeze.

Then Papa saw,
as he rounded a bend,
that the cave was open
at the other end.

At first Pa was blinded
by the sudden light.
But, when, in a moment
he recovered his sight,
he was astonished
by what he observed.
He was truly amazed,
completely unnerved.
For what was going on —
was BASEBALL!

That's right —
to Papa Bear's great surprise,
it was a baseball field
that greeted his eyes.

Not much of one,
but he had to confess,
a baseball field,
nevertheless.

As he watched the game
get under way,
Pa thought back
to another day,
where rain or shine,
sun or shade,
on this very backwoods
field he'd played.

When bats were sticks,
and umps were bats,
and no one kept
scores or stats.

Strike!

When a tree stump
served as second base,

and they had an extra
ball in case
their baseball
came unraveled
as through the country
air it traveled.

As now, it was
all lumps and bumps,
not to mention
rocks and stumps.

So bad hops were
half the fun.
"Look! Someone just hit
a bad hop home run!"

As he watched, a thought
came on strong:
he'd been wrong
all along!

Baseball's not a path
to glory and fame!
F-U-N, fun
is the name
of the game!

So Pa saw the error
of his ways.
And over the next
couple of days,
without any grown-up
pressure or nagging,
without any Papa Bear
boasting or bragging,
Pa stayed on the beam
and put together a
good baseball team.
But, the team had one
serious lack.
It was very weak
at the keystone sack.

"For our team," said Pa,
"to stay in the race,
we're going to need a glove
at second base."

Papa tried every cub in sight. Well, not quite *every* cub in sight.

That's when Papa finally saw the light.

"Sister Bear, take the field!" At second she was an impenetrable shield.

She stopped bounders and grounders and liners, too.

Absolutely *nothing* got through.

"Tremendous!" cried Pa,
quite carried away,
"Hooray for Sister!
Hip, hip, hooray!

She'll be the first
female superstar!
Revolutionize the game!
Go down in baseball history!
Make the Hall of Fame!"

Oops! Sorry about that everyone.

And the cubs got back
to baseball fun!
Great big, capital

F-U-N, FUN!

•ABOUT THE AUTHORS•

Stan and Jan Berenstain have been writing and illustrating books about bears for more than thirty years. In 1962, their self-proclaimed "mom and pop operation" began producing one of the most popular children's book series of all time—*The Berenstain Bears*. Since then, children the world over have followed Mama Bear, Papa Bear, Sister Bear, and Brother Bear on over 100 adventures through books, cassettes, and animated television specials.

Stan and Jan Berenstain live in Bucks County, Pennsylvania. They have two sons, Michael and Leo, and four grandchildren.